THIS BLOOMSBURY BOOK

BELONGS TO

....

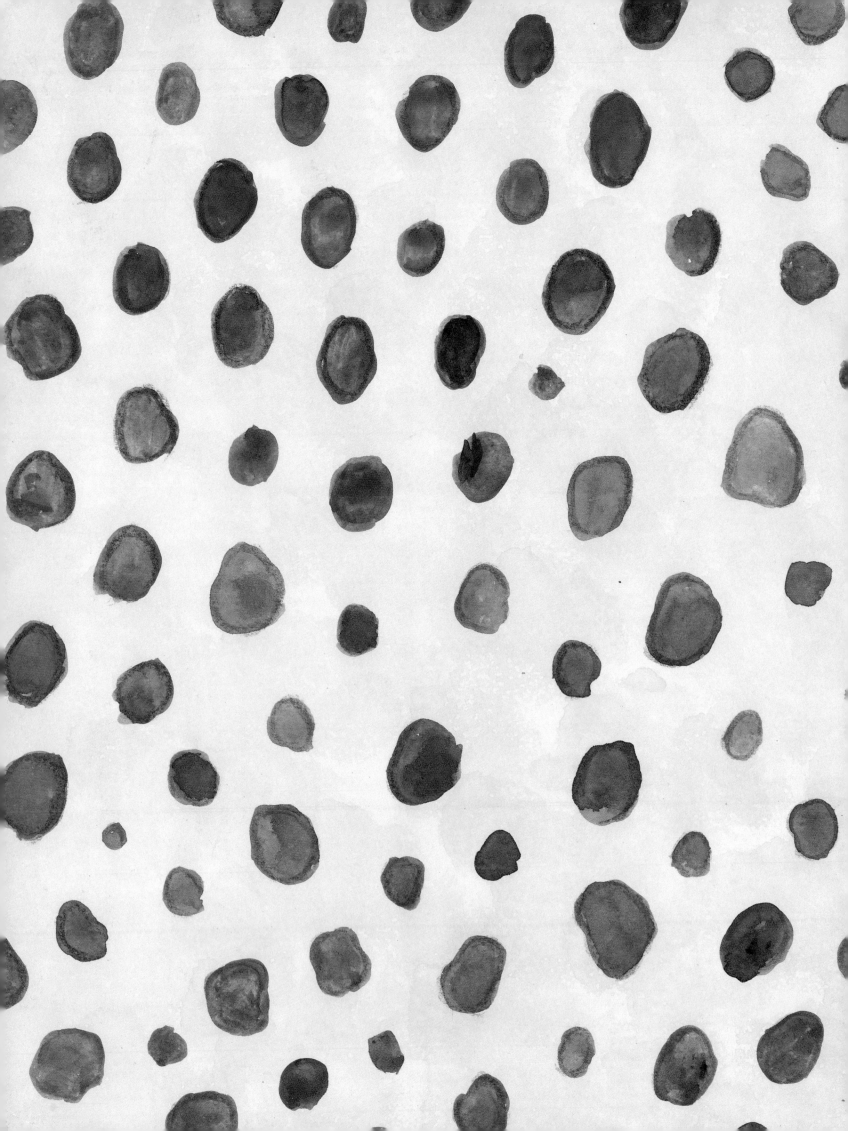

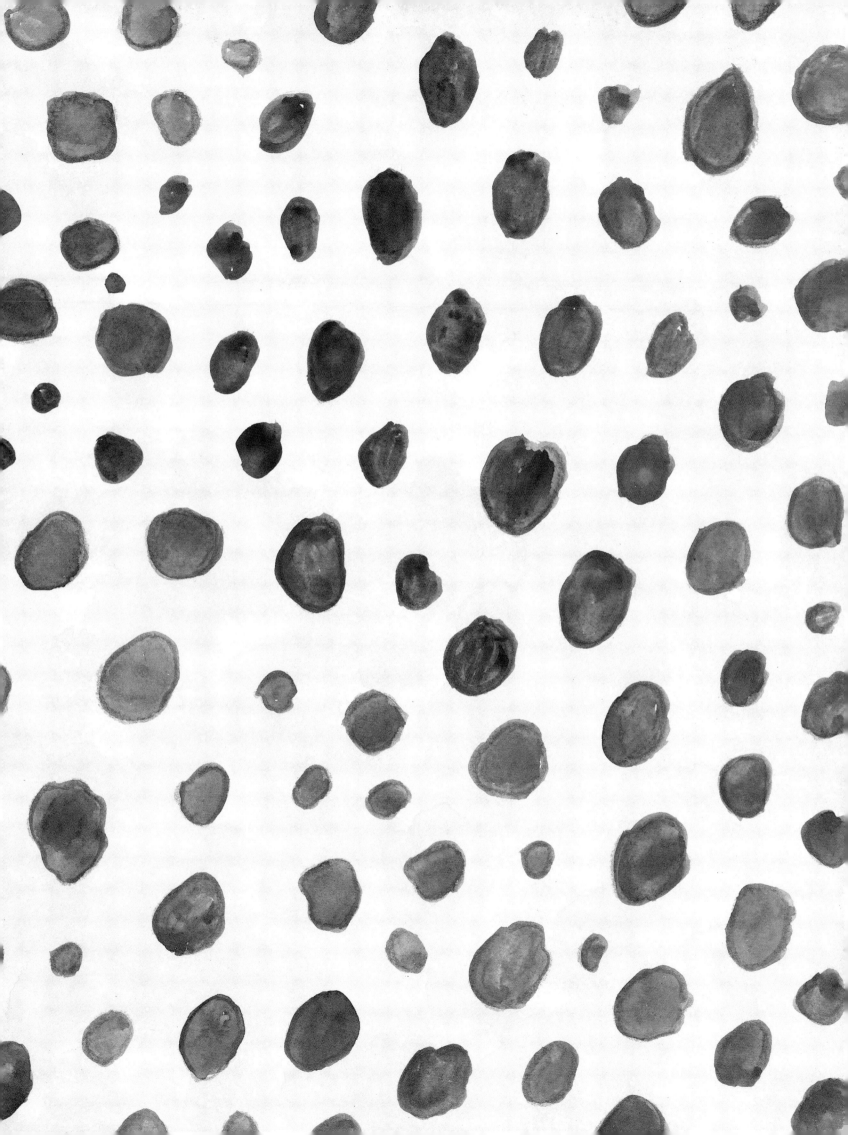

For my Mum and Dad,
and anyone else who just never
quite gets round to tidying up.

First published in Great Britain in 2000 by Bloomsbury Publishing Plc
38 Soho Square, London W1V 5DF
This paperback edition first published in 2001

Text and illustrations copyright © Dawn Apperley 2000
The moral right of the author has been asserted.

A CIP catalogue record for this book is available from the British Library.
ISBN 0 7475 5023 9 (paperback)
ISBN 0 7475 4474 3 (hardback)

Designed by Dawn Apperley

Printed and bound in Singapore by Tien Wah Press

5 7 9 10 8 6 4

There's an Octopus Under my Bed!

Dawn Apperley

BLOOMSBURY
CHILDREN'S
BOOKS

Molly didn't like tidying up.

On Monday Molly was dancing in her palace,
when her mother said,

'Molly, tidy up!'

But she was too busy being a princess.
Then Molly went for tea, and she still
hadn't tidied up.

When she came back, the palace had disappeared. Her bedroom was tidy. Molly didn't understand. She'd only been gone a few minutes.

'It's magicness,' thought Molly.

On Tuesday Molly was pony jumping, when
her mother said,
'Molly, tidy up!'
But she was too busy hopping around the
racetrack.

Then Molly went for tea, and she still hadn't tidied up.

When she came back, the racetrack had vanished. The garden was tidy. 'Something with a lot of arms is tidying up,' thought Molly.

On Wednesday Molly was making a special sea perfume, when her mother said,

'Molly, tidy up!'

But she was too busy mixing her potion. Then Molly went for tea, and she still hadn't tidied up.

When she came back, the
perfume factory had moved.
The bathroom was tidy.
'It must be an octopus,'
thought Molly.

On Thursday Molly was building a dinosaur,
when her mother said,
'Molly, tidy up!'

But Molly was too busy having fun with
Stegosaurus.
Then Molly went for tea, and she still hadn't
tidied up.

When Molly came back, the living room
was tidy.
'I'd like to meet Octopus,' she thought.

Molly looked under her bed, in the hose,

down the toilet and even inside the top drawer!

But Molly couldn't find Octopus anywhere.
Then she had an idea...

On Friday, when her mother said,
'Molly, tidy up!'

Molly carried on performing gymnastics,
making an enormous mess of her bedroom.
And when Molly went for tea,
she ate it super fast,
and raced back to her bedroom.

Molly imagined Octopus would be incredibly
busy today because she'd left a huge mess,
even for her.

Boy, did she have a surprise...

... it was her mother!

So on Saturday, when her mother said,
'Molly, tidy up!'

She did.

Well, sort of...

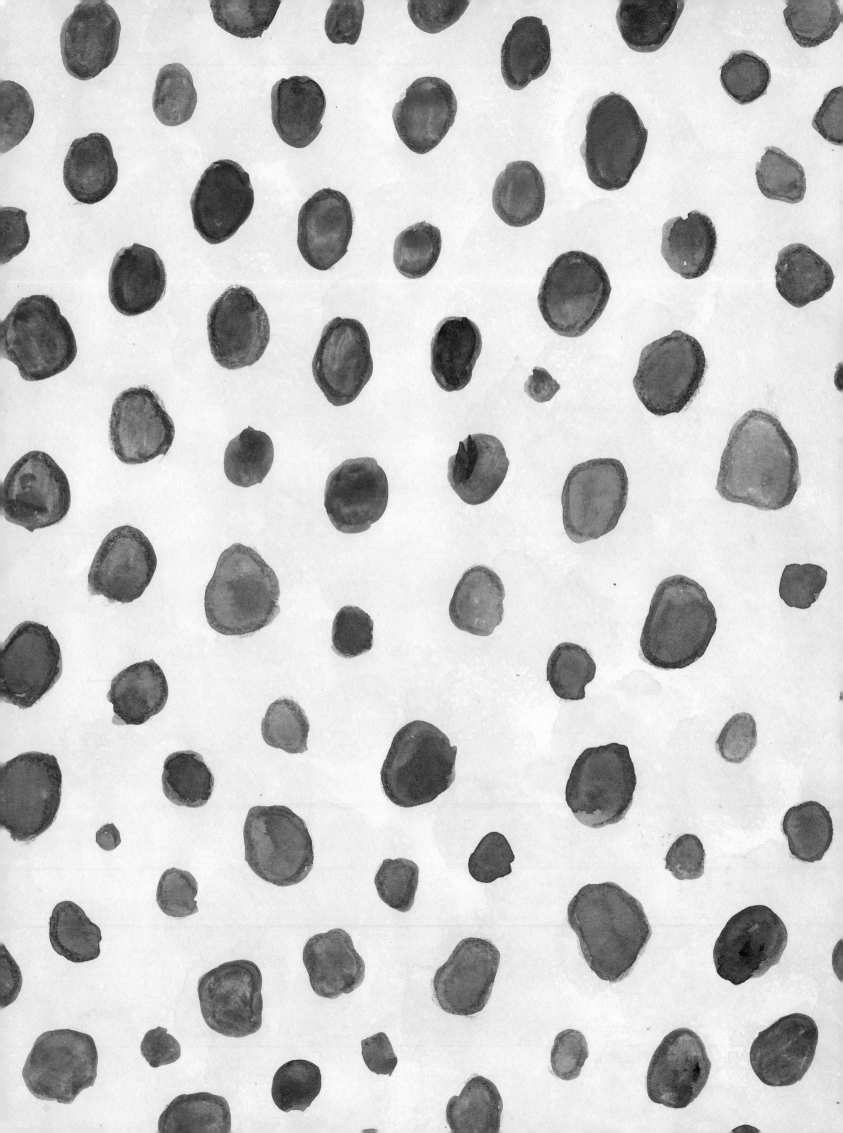

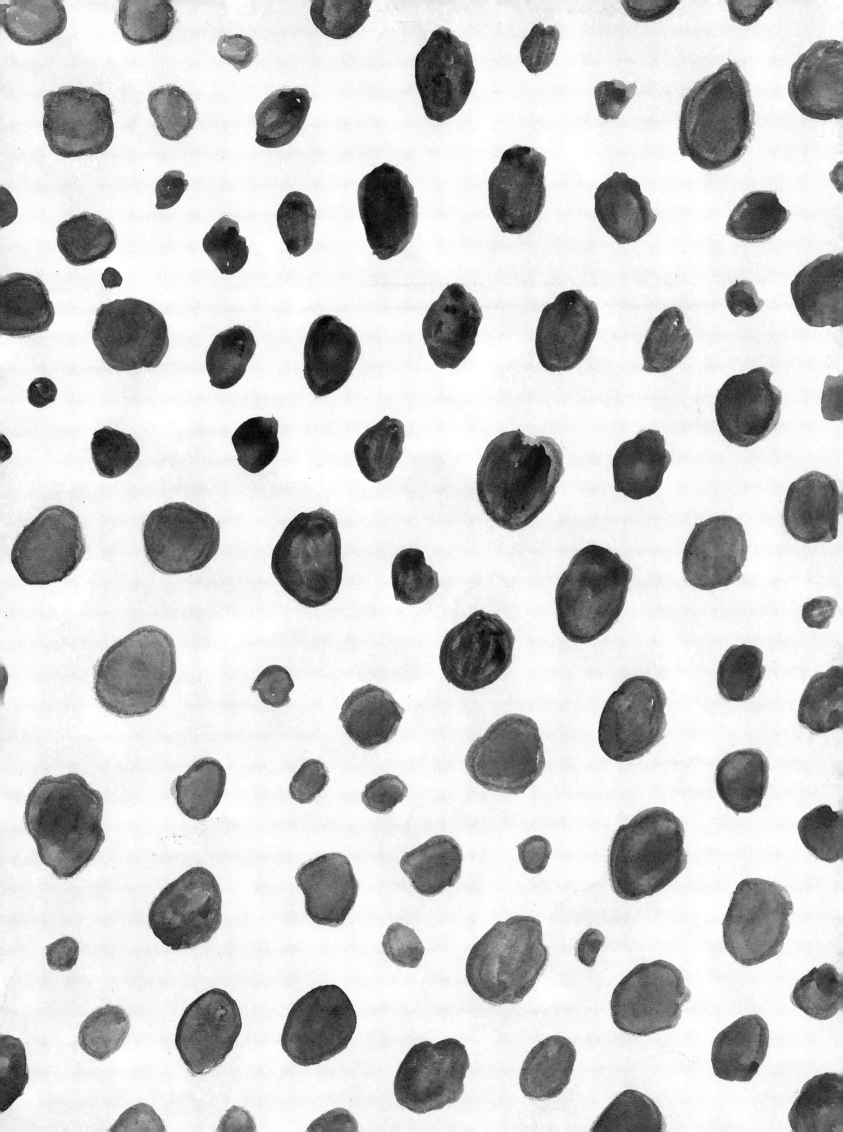